Acting Edition

Ken Ludwig's 'Twas the Night Before Christmas

SAMUEL FRENCH

Copyright © 2013 by Ken Ludwig. All Rights Reserved.
Cover Image Courtesy of Adventure Theatre MTC
All Rights Reserved

KEN LUDWIG'S 'TWAS THE NIGHT BEFORE CHRISTMAS is fully protected under the copyright laws of the United States of America, the British Commonwealth, including Canada, and all member countries of the Berne Convention for the Protection of Literary and Artistic Works, the Universal Copyright Convention, and/or the World Trade Organization conforming to the Agreement on Trade Related Aspects of Intellectual Property Rights. All rights, including professional and amateur stage productions, recitation, lecturing, public reading, motion picture, radio broadcasting, television, online/digital production, and the rights of translation into foreign languages are strictly reserved.

ISBN 978-0-573-66341-3

www.concordtheatricals.com
www.concordtheatricals.co.uk

FOR PRODUCTION INQUIRIES

UNITED STATES AND CANADA
info@concordtheatricals.com
1-866-979-0447

UNITED KINGDOM AND EUROPE
licensing@concordtheatricals.co.uk
020-7054-7298

Each title is subject to availability from Concord Theatricals Corp., depending upon country of performance. Please be aware that *KEN LUDWIG'S 'TWAS THE NIGHT BEFORE CHRISTMAS* may not be licensed by Concord Theatricals Corp. in your territory. Professional and amateur producers should contact the nearest Concord Theatricals Corp. office or licensing partner to verify availability.

CAUTION: Professional and amateur producers are hereby warned that *KEN LUDWIG'S 'TWAS THE NIGHT BEFORE CHRISTMAS* is subject to a licensing fee. The purchase, renting, lending or use of this book does not constitute a license to perform this title(s), which license must be obtained from Concord Theatricals Corp. prior to any performance. Performance of this title(s) without a license is a violation of federal law and may subject the producer and/or presenter of such performances to civil penalties. Both amateurs and professionals considering a production are strongly advised to apply to the appropriate agent before starting rehearsals, advertising, or booking a theatre. A licensing fee must be paid whether the title(s) is presented for charity or gain and whether or not admission is charged. Professional/Stock licensing fees are quoted upon application to Concord Theatricals Corp.

This work is published by Samuel French, an imprint of Concord Theatricals Corp.

No one shall make any changes in this title(s) for the purpose of production. No part of this book may be reproduced, stored in a retrieval system, scanned, uploaded, or transmitted in any form, by any means, now known or yet to be invented, including mechanical, electronic, digital, photocopying, recording, videotaping, or otherwise, without the prior written permission of the publisher. No one shall share this title(s), or any part of this title(s), through any social media or file hosting websites.

For all inquiries regarding motion picture, television, online/digital and other media rights, please contact Concord Theatricals Corp.

MUSIC AND THIRD-PARTY MATERIALS USE NOTE

Licensees are solely responsible for obtaining formal written permission from copyright owners to use copyrighted music and/or other copyrighted third-party materials (e.g. artworks, logos) in the performance of this play and are strongly cautioned to do so. If no such permission is obtained by the licensee, then the licensee must use only original music and materials that the licensee owns and controls. Licensees are solely responsible and liable for clearances of all third-party copyrighted materials, including without limitation music, and shall indemnify the copyright owners of the play(s) and their licensing agent, Concord Theatricals Corp., against any costs, expenses, losses and liabilities arising from the use of such copyrighted third-party materials by licensees. For music, please contact the appropriate music licensing authority in your territory for the rights to any incidental music.

IMPORTANT BILLING AND CREDIT REQUIREMENTS

If you have obtained performance rights to this title, please refer to your licensing agreement for important billing and credit requirements.

All producers of *KEN LUDWIG'S 'TWAS THE NIGHT BEFORE CHRISTMAS* must give credit to the Author(s) of the Play(s) in all programs distributed in connection with performances of the Play(s), and in all instances in which the title of the Play(s) appears for the purposes of advertising, publicizing or otherwise exploiting the Play(s) and/or a production. The name of the Author(s) must appear on a separate line on which no other name appears, immediately above the title and must appear in size of type not less than seventy-five percent of the size of the title type. The title should read:

In addition the following credit must be given in all programs and publicity information distributed in association with this piece:

Ken Ludwig's 'TWAS THE NIGHT BEFORE CHRISTMAS
Originally commissioned
by Adventure Theatre, Glen Echo, MD
Michael J. Bobbitt, Producing Artistic Director

KEN LUDWIG'S 'TWAS THE NIGHT BEFORE CHRISTMAS was first presented by Adventure Theatre (Michael Bobbitt, Artistic Director), in Washington DC on November 20, 2011. The performance was directed by Jerry Whiddon, with sets by Luciana Stecconi, lighting by Andrew F. Griffin, sound by Brandon Roe, costumes by Chelsey Schuller, movement and choreography by Karen Abromaitis, and music direction by Wayne Chadwick. The cast was as follows:

SIR GUY OF GISBOURNE/UNCLE BRIERLY. . . . . .Gary Sloan

AMOS/AMOS OF KANSAS . . . . Rex Daugherty

EMILY . . . . .Emily Levey

CALLIOPE/BRITANNIA SNEED. Rachel Zampelli

MULCH/SANTA CLAUS/WENDELL SNEED. . . . . .Alex Perez

CHARACTERS

SIR GUY OF GISBOURNE / UNCLE BRIERLY

AMOS / AMOS OF KANSAS

EMILY

CALLIOPE / BRITANNIA SNEED

MULCH / SANTA CLAUS / WENDELL SNEED

(Note: Amos and Amos of Kansas are boy mice and were played by an actor in the original production. They could, however, be played by an actress, as a trouser role – still boy mice, but played by a woman. So the cast is either 3 female and 2 male, or 2 female and 3 male.)

SETTING

In the text of the play, the action begins in a house in Vermont; however each production can be set locally. Thus the reference in the first stage direction can use the state or city name where the theater is located.

Scene One

(The time is Christmas Eve, and at the moment we're in the well-preserved living room of the Brittleback's home at the end of a cheerful, snowy lane in Vermont. Christmas is beautiful everywhere, but it is especially beautiful in an old-fashioned living room with oriental rugs on a hardwood floor, windows looking out to trees laden with fresh snow so heavy that the branches of the trees bow down almost to the ground; a roaring fire with a grate full of glowing embers; and a Christmas tree covered in lights and ornaments that soars to the top of the timbered ceiling and seems to travel right on up to the sky.)

(As the audience settles down, **UNCLE BRIERLY** *enters. He is middle-aged and a bit portly, wearing a tartan vest and a knotted Windsor tie; he has a plummy, resonant voice and a hearty manner; and when he beams at the children he could be the kindly uncle of any one of them, just the sort of man you want to see at Christmas time.)*

(And yet…there's something slightly off-kilter about this moment, this house and this man. Perhaps it's because this is a magical time of year. Or perhaps it's because the people in this house believe in their hearts that Santa Claus is no less real than any one of them. To them he is not a myth, nor is this house or this season a myth. They are all Believers here, and so are we.)

UNCLE BRIERLY. *(entering, calling back into the room he's coming from)* I'll be right back! Enjoy the party in there! Just thought I'd give the kiddies out here a little Christmas poem, that's all! Ha ha!

(He turns and sees the children in the audience.)

UNCLE BRIERLY. *(cont.)* Ah. Children. There you are. Good afternoon and welcome all of you on this snowy and wonderful Christmas Eve to this magnificent home, and may I say to every one of you: *Merry Christmas!* I'm now going to recite for you my favorite poem of all time, one that I'm sure you've never heard before, "*'Twas The Night Before Christmas*." Ahem.

(He clears his throat and Christmas music begins to play in the background, the kind with jingling sleigh bells, evoking a ride in the country behind a trotting horse. The opening of the first movement of Mahler's 4th Symphony would do nicely. Perhaps a bit of snow falls from above and dusts **UNCLE BRIERLY**'s *shoulders.)*

"'Twas the night before Christmas when all through the house,
Not a creature was stirring, not even a mouse."

(At which moment a mouse enters holding a bowl in his arm, stirring the contents with a wooden spoon. The mouse's name is **AMOS**.*)*

AMOS. Hold it! Hold it! Stop the presses! You got it wrong!

UNCLE BRIERLY. I beg your pardon! Who are you? And *what* are you?

AMOS. What do I look like? I'm a mouse. I live here. Now look at me carefully. What am I doin'?

UNCLE BRIERLY. I have no idea.

AMOS. I'm stirring. See? I'm makin' cookies for Santa Claus, so I'm *stirring the batter*. Stir, stir, stir, stir.

UNCLE BRIERLY. So?

AMOS. So you fibbed to all those nice little children out there. You said "Not a creature was stirring, not even a mouse." But I'm a mouse and I'm stirring. Stir, stir, stir, stir.

UNCLE BRIERLY. That's not the kind of stirring I was talking about. The word "stirring" can also mean "moving" – "not a creature was *moving*" – and I was using it in that sense, to describe a house where everything is *quiet* on Christmas eve like this house should be now may I *continue?*

AMOS. Okay. If you feel you gotta. Whatever floats your boat.

(**AMOS** *stands to the side, watching and stirring.*)

UNCLE BRIERLY. Ahem. Twasthenightbeforechristmasand allthroughthehousenotacreasurewasstirringnotevena mouse. ...Right.

(*The music and the snow return happily again.*)

"The stockings were hung by the chimney with care,
In hopes that Saint Nicholas soon would be there."

AMOS. (*to himself*) "Hopes" is right, Mister. Let's "hope" that Santa makes it to the house this time. Just get yourself down that chimney, baby-face, that's all I'm askin', down the old...

(**UNCLE BRIERLY** *is staring at him.*)

sorry.

UNCLE BRIERLY. ..."The children were nestled all snug in their beds,
While visions of sugar plums danced in their heads."

(**AMOS** *starts dancing and humming to himself. He's now holding a stuffed animal – a pigeon – and he dances with it.*)

AMOS. Dya dum de daaaaa, dya da da da da da daaaaaaa...

UNCLE BRIERLY. What are you doing?

AMOS. I'm dancing.

UNCLE BRIERLY. Why are you dancing?

AMOS. I'm a sugar plum. Dya dum de daaaaa, dya da da da da da –

UNCLE BRIERLY. You are *not* a sugar plum. A sugar plum is a piece of candy. Are you a piece of candy?

AMOS. No.

UNCLE BRIERLY. And what is *that*?

AMOS. A pigeon.

UNCLE BRIERLY. Yes, I see it's a pigeon, but why are you dancing with it?

AMOS. Because you said "while pigeons and sugar plums danced in their heads."

UNCLE BRIERLY. No, I didn't. I said, "*visions of sugar plums.*" Not pigeons and sugar plums. Why would a sugar plum dance with a pigeon?

AMOS. Why would a piece of candy dance at all?

UNCLE BRIERLY. Because it's Christmas Eve!

AMOS. You're tellin' me. That's why I'm makin' these cookies for Santa. So he'll come to our house this year.

UNCLE BRIERLY. He comes every year.

AMOS. He didn't come last year.

UNCLE BRIERLY. Of course he did.

AMOS. No he didn't.

UNCLE BRIERLY. He did.

AMOS. He didn't.

UNCLE BRIERLY. Did!

AMOS. *Didn't! He missed our house! And I wanted a squirt gun and I didn't get it!*

UNCLE BRIERLY. *(overlapping) He comes every year! He's Santa Claus! He doesn't forget things!*

(**EMILY** *runs in. She's a sweet little girl with attitude, about ten years old.*)

EMILY. Uncle Brierly! Stop yelling! What's going on?!

UNCLE BRIERLY. This-this-this mouse is driving me crazy! Oh – now don't be frightened. He's just a rodent. I'll call the exterminator.

AMOS. Hi, Emily.

EMILY. Hi, Amos.

(*They do a hand-greeting.*)

UNCLE BRIERLY. You…you *know* him?

EMILY. Of course I know him. He's my best friend. We grew up together. Remember that time I broke my tooth? It was Amos who brought me the ice cream and fed it to me.

AMOS. *(proudly)* Chocolate Broccoli.

EMILY. And that time I fell off my bicycle? It was Amos who ran and got the bandaid. Then he spit on my knee and put it right on top!

AMOS. Aw, it was nothin'.

EMILY. And he taught me to swim, and use a napkin, and eat Swiss cheese without eating the holes -

UNCLE BRIERLY. All right, all right! I get the picture! What's that?

AMOS. The picture. See, there's me, there's Emily…

UNCLE BRIERLY. *Would you stop that!*

EMILY. Uncle Brierly, don't yell at him. You'll hurt his feelings.

UNCLE BRIERLY. I can't help it. He's driving me crazy! First he's stirring, then he's dancing –

AMOS. I'm a happy person.

UNCLE BRIERLY. You're not a person at all, you're a mouse.

AMOS. Oh, thank you for telling me, like I didn't notice.

*(At this moment, **WENDELL SNEED** enters like a tsunami. He's **BRIERLY**'s age, a big, bluff, noisy, good-natured fellow who's been invited to the party and is delighted to see his old friend.)*

WENDELL. *(entering)* Brierly? Brier-leeeeeee! Ha ha! How are you, old man? How long has it *Britannia! (He's calling to his wife, **BRITANNIA**, who's off stage.) Look who's here! Come quickly!*

UNCLE BRIERLY. Hello, Wendell. Good to see you. Thank you for –

WENDELL. Wonderful party! Food. Drink. Children. I'm delighted to *Britannia! Don't dawdle! Brierly's here!*

*(**BRITANNIA** enters. She's **WENDELL**'s wife and just as dotty.)*

BRITANNIA. Yes, dear, I'm coming, I'm *coming!* He's always in such a *Brierly! How marvelous after all this* Wendell, you didn't tell me he was here.

WENDELL. Of course he's here, it's his brother's house! How could Brierly not be How do you do. Hello. *(This was to* **EMILY.***)* I'm Wendell. My wife Britannia.

EMILY. How do you do?

UNCLE BRIERLY. My niece, Emily. Emily, the Sneeds.

AMOS. Bless you.

UNCLE BRIERLY. I didn't sneeze. I said the Sneeds!

AMOS. Bless you!

UNCLE BRIERLY. The Sneeds!

AMOS. Bless you! *(pulls out a handkerchief)* Don't you want to wipe your nose after all that?

UNCLE BRIERLY. *Would you stop it!*

WENDELL. Hello. I'm Wendell Sneed and this is –

BRITANNIA. Britannia. How do you do, it's enchanting to meet you.

AMOS. How do you do. Amos Mouse

UNCLE BRIERLY. *"KIN!" Mousekin.* Amos Mousekin. He's the *son*, you see, of a friend of the family. Not a rodent at all. No, no. The tail – it's a costume. Nothing mousey about him.

EMILY. Oh, stop it, Uncle. He is a mouse, and he's my best friend. We play together all the time.

WENDELL. Like Brierly and I used to do, eh? Ha! Ha ha! We played in the woods, the fields, you name it, we played there – cowboys – Indians – *Robin Hood!* That was our favorite.

UNCLE BRIERLY. *(lovingly)* Robin Hood.

WENDELL. I played Much the Miller's son and Brierly played the villain of course. Oh what was his name, Sir Gee, Sir Goo –

UNCLE BRIERLY. Sir Guy.

WENDELL. That's it! He was Sir Guy of Gisbourne. The wickedest villain who ever *Hya! Hya! Hya!*

BRITANNIA. Oh, what fun! Now *my* friends and I played a different game, we called it "Save the Elf!" We all pretended to be Santa's elves and make toys in the Workshop.

EMILY. The Workshop?! Really? Oh, I'd *love* to see Santa's Workshop. I dream about it all the time when I fall asleep, I really do. But even if it *does* exist I'll never see it now that Santa's forgotten about us …

WENDELL. Forgotten?

BRITANNIA. He's forgotten you?

WENDELL. That's awful!

BRITANNIA. That's terrible!

UNCLE BRIERLY. That's preposterous!

EMILY. No, it's true, Uncle. You see last Christmas Santa visited all the other houses in the neighborhood, but he didn't come here.

AMOS. *(sadly)* Which means he'll probably miss us again this year.

EMILY. *(sniff)* And the year after that.

AMOS. *(sniff sniff)* And the year after that and every year till we get really, really old like your Uncle Brierly!

(He points at **UNCLE BRIERLY** *and they both start crying loudly.)*

AMOS & EMILY. *Ahhhhhhh!*

BRITANNIA. I think we'd better –

WENDELL. – go, of course, you're right, it's time for us to

BRITANNIA. Off we go.

WENDELL. We're gone.

BRITANNIA. No more.

WENDELL. We vanish, poof.

BRITANNIA. Bye-bye.

(And they're gone. Beat. **AMOS** *and* **EMILY** *look at* **UNCLE BRIERLY**…*and burst into tears again.)*

BOTH. *Whaaaaaaaaaaa!*

UNCLE BRIERLY. All right, that's it! I've had it! Anyone who wants to stay here with my niece and this hysterical mouse may do so. But I have to warn you, they are *young.* When people are young they don't use good judgment. They take chances, which is silly, and they make mistakes, which is even sillier. They should be level-headed, the way adults are. Look at me. I never make mistakes, and I don't do things that are silly! *Ow!*

(He has rapped his cane on the ground to emphasize his point and has hit his toe by accident.)

UNCLE BRIERLY. *(cont.)* Ooh, ow, ooh, ow! Children will tell you they take chances because it's all part of growing up, but that's nonsense. You will grow up either way. That's what Nature is for. It pulls you to heaven. I never took a single chance in my entire life and as you can see, I AM PERFECTLY HAPPY! *(He isn't.) Now* – for those who would like to hear the end of the greatest poem ever written, follow me!

(He turns and exits through a door at the back of the set but walks into the wall or walks out the door and into something.)

Ow!

EMILY. Good-bye, Uncle Brierly! I'm sorry if we hurt your –

(Too late; he's gone.)

He means well. He's just old-fashioned. I mean, if you're going to recite *The Night Before Christmas*, you really ought to express yourself.

AMOS. Modernize.

EMILY. Hypothesize.

AMOS. And *vitalize!*

(Rock/rap music starts to throb and **EMILY** *and* **AMOS** *start dancing and singing:)*

EMILY & **AMOS**.
"'TWAS THE NIGHT BEFORE CHRISTMAS AND ALL THROUGH
    THE HOUSE,
NOT A CREATURE WAS STIRRING
NOT A CREATURE WAS STIRRING
NOT A CREATURE WAS STIRRING NOT EVEN A MOUSE!
A MOUSE, A MOUSE,

IN THE HOUSE
LIKE A RAT
ON THE MAT
HANG ONTO YOUR HAT, 'CAUSE THE
STOCKINGS WERE HUNG BY THE CHIMNEY WITH CARE,
IN THE HOPES THAT SAINT NICK,
IN THE HOPES THAT SAINT NICK,
SAINT NICK, SAINT NICK,
GOTTA BE MIGHTY QUICK,
AND HE'S GOTTA BE SLICK,
TO DO THAT CHIMNEY TRICK.
HE'S QUICK, HE'S SLICK,
WITH THE CHIMNEY MADE O' BRICK,
'CAUSE HE'S BRINGIN' HIS TOYS,
AND HE'S MAKIN' SOME NOISE
FOR THE GIRLS AND THE BOYS
WITH A BAG FULLA JOYS
'CAUSE HE'S SANTA
DRINKIN' FANTA
MR. CLAUS BECAUSE
BECAUSE BECAUSE
HE'S SANTA
AND HE CAN'T A–
COME LATE
COMIN' EARLY
IN THE PEARLY
MORNIN' LIGHT
NOT LATE
WE'LL WAIT
FOR THE MAN WITH THE BEARD
AND THE BAG
WITH THE SWAG
CHERRY NOSE
THAT'S HOW IT GOES
BLACK BOOT
AND THE BRIGHT RED SUIT!

(When the number's over, **EMILY** *sees something:)*

EMILY. AHHHHHHHHHH!

(**EMILY** *has just seen an elf looking through one of the windows. When* **EMILY** *screams, the head disappears from view.*)

Who's that!

AMOS. What?

EMILY. That!

AMOS. Where?

EMILY. There!

AMOS. Who?

EMILY. Her!

AMOS. Why?

EMILY. Why not?

AMOS. Good point.

EMILY. She's gone! Didn't you see her?! There was a girl or something at the window. She looked sort of … otherworldly. Holy cow, I think she was an elf!

AMOS. An elf? Don't be ridiculous.

(*At which moment, the elf's head reappears.* **EMILY** *sees it but* **AMOS** *doesn't, so he keeps talking.*)

Elves don't come to Vermont. They live at the North Pole with Santa Claus. Besides, they're so busy makin' toys they don't have time to travel around and –

EMILY. Look!

AMOS. What?

EMILY. That!

AMOS. Where?

EMILY. There!

AMOS. Who?

EMILY. Her!

AMOS. Her who?!

EMILY. That that!!…She's gone again.

AMOS. She is? Oh good! Now I don't have to meet her.

(Bing Bong!)

EMILY. Holy Hannah!

AMOS. Who's Hannah?

EMILY. I have no idea, but I think she's at the door. I'll be right back. But don't worry. If she's big and scary with enormous teeth and blood-shot eyes, I'll just tell her we're not home.

(She heads off.)

AMOS. Wait! Don't leave me! What if it's that…teeth and… eyes and…

(AMOS *turns to the audience.)*

I know this is gonna surprise you, but I'm not a brave mouse. I mean I act brave, and I look brave, but inside I'm like, "I don't want to meet strange people. I don't want to leave my safe little house." And I sure don't want to meet some scary elf with pointy ears who flies around on a reindeer or something. When I even think about flying, my fur stands on end like a pin cushion. Which is not to say I can't be forceful when I have to be. Or strong, or *tough!* I'm not a scaredy-cat. I'm not a cat at all. I can be as brave as any mouse in the entire –

CALLIOPE. *(entering)* Hello.

AMOS. *YAHHHHHHHHH!*

(EMILY *reenters with an elf named* **CALLIOPE** *who is dressed in a trench coat and has a fedora pulled down over her face.* **AMOS** *is shaking like a leaf.)*

EMILY. Please come in.

CALLIOPE. *(using a deep voice, being very "official")* How do you do, how do you do. I'm here from the government.

EMILY. The government?!

CALLIOPE. I'm with the Elf-B-I. We ask questions. We get to the bottom of things. For example, do you live here?

BOTH. Yes./Yes, we do.

CALLIOPE. *(writing it down)* Good, good. And what did Santa bring you last year for Christmas?

AMOS. He didn't come last year.

CALLIOPE. He didn't?

BOTH. No./Nope.

CALLIOPE. Are you sure?

BOTH. Yep./Uh-huh.

CALLIOPE. *(throwing off her coat and hat)* I *knew it!* That is *just what I thought! I was right!*

AMOS. Oh my gosh!

EMILY. You *are* an elf!!

*(She is an elf, a Christmas elf, with pointy ears. She takes off her coat and we see that she's wearing a green jerkin and tights with sparkles on them and a Robin Hood-type hat with a feather. She's 518 years old but she looks like she's 14 and a half. Her name is **CALLIOPE**.)*

AMOS. *(agog)* Are you a Christmas elf?

CALLIOPE. That's right. How do you do. My name's Calliope.

EMILY. Emily.

AMOS. Wow! A real elf! And look at your necklace. Is that like a symbol for the North Pole or something?

CALLIOPE. No, it's called a Star of David. I'm a Jewish elf. There are five of us in all. We don't work on Friday nights.

AMOS. This is the best day of my life!

CALLIOPE. Mazel Tov.

AMOS. Mazelwhat?

CALLIOPE. Now listen to me, I need your help. We have an emergency at the North Pole and you're the only two people in the world who can help us!

AMOS. I'm not a people.

CALLIOPE. Don't get technical. You see, I've suspected for almost a year now that *this house* was somehow taken off the Naughty-and-Nice List just before Santa started his rounds last Christmas. But the problem is, he doesn't believe me. He thinks that everything is hunky-dory – Santa always thinks everything is hunky-dory – but *I* think there's something funny going on.

AMOS. Funny ha-ha or funny *yulhhhhh.*

CALLIOPE. Funny *yulhhhh.* So you two have to tell Santa that he *didn't* visit here last Christmas because then he'll believe it and he'll *do* something about it. Now let's go.

EMILY. Go?

AMOS. Go where?

CALLIOPE. To the North Pole so you can tell Santa! Now come on!

AMOS. *(politely)* Uh, excuse me. When you say, "the North Pole," you mean that place about ten thousand miles from here where they have the glaciers and hungry polar bears and you can lose your fingers 'cause they freeze and then fall off like little ice sculptures?

CALLIOPE. Yeah, that's it.

AMOS. I see. …*ARE YOU CRAZY?! ARE YOU NUTS?! HAVE YOU LOST YOUR LITTLE ELFIN MIND?!!!*

EMILY. But Amos, this is important!

AMOS. So is my life important! And-and-and-and how are we supposed to get there, huh?! Use *pixie dust?!*

CALLIOPE. As a matter of fact, I'm out of pixie dust, so we'll have to fly.

AMOS. "Fly"? Oh, oh, oh, that's great. So what do you think, I'm a bird now? Huh? *(He holds up his tail.)* Does this tail look like a *wing* to you?! Cause I know this is gonna surprise you, but I CAN'T FLY!

CALLIOPE. Look, don't you understand that Christmas is at stake?! If you don't help me, there'll be no Christmas for kids all over the world like you and you and him and her, *(i.e. two kids in the audience)* now would you please stop making excuses and *come on!*

(CALLIOPE hurries out.)

AMOS. Polar bears…icicles…my fingers…

EMILY. Oh, Amos, don't be scared. We have to do this. And just think, some day we can tell our children about it!

(**EMILY** *hurries out.*)

AMOS. Children? I'm ten years old. I am a children. *(calling to her)* And I don't even like adventures!

I like my house. I like my bed. I like those nice warm covers that I can snuggle into every –

EMILY. *(off) Amos, hurry up!*

(From out on the lawn we hear the engine of a small airplane sputter into life. Amos runs and looks out the window.)

AMOS. An airplane? It looks like a crop-duster! Oh, I'm not gonna like this…

CALLIOPE. *(off) Amos, come on!*

AMOS. *All right, I'm coming! Geronimoooooooooooo!*

(And he runs out the door.)

Scene Two

*(As **AMOS** disappears, the sound of the biplane gets louder and louder – and soon we're looking at the front half of the plane as it flies through a cloud. **CALLIOPE** is in the cockpit, flying the plane, and **AMOS** and **EMILY** are right behind her. They all wear goggles, and **CALLIOPE** wears a jaunty flying scarf.)*

EMILY. Wow, just look at all those tiny people down there.

CALLIOPE. This is fun, isn't it!

AMOS. *(terrified) Ah ah ah ah put on the brakes, tell it to stop! I'm not a flyer, I'm not a flyer!*

EMILY. Can you go upside-down?

CALLIOPE. Sure, no problem! Do you want me to spin it?!

EMILY. Yeah!

AMOS. *No, no! No! Don't! Don't do it!*

EMILY. Oh, Amos, stop being silly. Flying is fun. It's as safe as walking.

AMOS. Fine, you fly, I'll walk. I'll see you later.

(He starts getting out of the plane.)

EMILY. *No, don't!!*

(She hauls him back in.)

Oh, look, there's a farm! It's so beautiful. And you were born in farm country, weren't you?

AMOS. I was, I was, but I never thought I'd see one from the top down. I like 'em sideways, with the cows and the ducks and the…

(Suddenly, a thought strikes him. This isn't an excuse: he's remembering something very important:)

Oh my gosh! Wait a second! "Farm country". Quick! Turn the plane around!

CALLIOPE. What?

AMOS. I'm not kiddin'. We gotta go back to the house *this second!*

EMILY. Amos, what's the matter?!

AMOS. My twin brother is comin' to visit today and I forgot all about it! He lives in Kansas and he's comin' to see me for Christmas!

EMILY. Amos –

AMOS. What'll I do?! He'll get to the house and I won't be there!

EMILY. Amos -

AMOS. He thinks I'm waitin' for him. Now I won't be there and he'll be scared to death!

EMILY. *Amos, he'll be fine!* I left a note for Uncle Brierly and I told him exactly where we were going, so he's bound to tell your brother, right?

AMOS. I guess…

CALLIOPE. What's your twin brother's name?

AMOS. Amos.

CALLIOPE. No, your *brother's* name.

AMOS. Amos. My mother thought it would be easier if we had the same name. She'd yell, "Hey, Amos!" and somebody would answer. People say we look alike but it's not true, I'm a lot handsomer. Ha ha! Hahahahahaha!

EMILY. You're having fun now, aren't you.

AMOS. Yeah, I suppose it's not so bad. In fact, it's pretty cool up here, if you want the truth. I mean look at all that snow down there. The trees are white, the houses are white, those two glaciers just ahead of us are white. I mean, you don't see things like that at home. Two huge glaciers without any room in between 'em and us just flyin' straight at 'em. …Hah… Us just…flyin'… straight down the middle?! *Ahh! What are you doin'?! Are you crazy?! There's hardly even a crack between those two humongous, mouse-destroying –*

CALLIOPE. *Hold on tight! We're going through sideways!!*

(*The engine roars and the plane banks so steeply that they're literally at a 90° angle to the ground.*)

EMILY. *Wheeeeee!*

AMOS. *Yaaaaaaaaaaaaaaaaaaaaahhhhh!*

(*THUMP! Transition to next scene:*)

AMOS. (*writhing around on the ground trying not to look*) *May Day! May Day! I surrender! May Day! Lemme outa the plane! Lemme outa the plane!*

EMILY. *Wait! I think we're all right!*

AMOS. *Hold on! Hold on! This thing could land any second!*

CALLIOPE. *It landed! Amos!*

EMILY. *You're still spinning!*

AMOS. *I'm not spinning, it's the plane that's spinning!*

EMILY. *Who's that?!*

CALLIOPE. *Where?!*

EMILY. *There!*

CALLIOPE. *I think it's the stage crew!*

(*It is: they're moving the set.*)

AMOS. *AHHH! WHAT'S A STAGE CREW!!*

CALLIOPE. *You don't want to know!*

AMOS. *I can hardly walk! I can hardly breathe! My head is numb! My fingers are numb! My teeth are numb!*

EMILY. *Amos, Amos! You're all right!*

CALLIOPE. *We're here!*

(*The three friends take a breath and look around.*)

Scene Three

(We're in Santa's Workshop. The transition music is the hunting walk from Tchaikovsky's Peter and the Wolf.*)*

(Santa's Workshop is a glorious place. As soon as we see it, it makes us feel happy. This might have to do with the workbenches made of chocolate, or the candy-cane tools or the gumdrop mirrors. Or it might be the dozens of colorful toys around the room in various states of completion. It might be that everything in the room has an inner glow like the heart of a child. Or it might just be that we've dreamed about this room all our lives and we're finally here.)

EMILY. Oh my gosh. It's Santa's Workshop, isn't it?

CALLIOPE. *(proudly)* Yeah, it is!

EMILY. Are these gumdrops?

AMOS. Is that a lollipop?

EMILY. They're enormous! May I?

CALLIOPE. Help yourselves.

EMILY. Sugar sugar sugar sugar –

AMOS. Sugar sugar sugar sugar –

EMILY. And oh wow! Look at all these toys! There are dolls by the hundreds!

AMOS. And trains.

EMILY. And trucks.

AMOS. And candy. Oh I love candy. *(He finds a candy bar.)* Can I kiss it?

CALLIOPE. …Wait a second…something's wrong. What time is it?

*(**AMOS** slaps his wrist and peers at it.)*

AMOS. I don't wear a watch.

EMILY. Calliope, what is it?

CALLIOPE. Normally this place is humming like a beehive. It's filled with elves and reindeer and everybody you can think of, so why is it empty? Oh my gosh, this isn't part of the plan.

AMOS. Plan?

EMILY. What plan?

AMOS. We have a plan?

SIR GUY. *(off) Mulch?! Mulch?!*

CALLIOPE. Shh! I hear somebody coming!

SIR GUY. *(off) Mulch, where are you?!*

MULCH. *(off) I'm coming, Sir Guy!*

CALLIOPE. Quick, let's hide!

> *(The three friends hide under the center workbench. During the following, we can see them reacting to the scene unfolding in front of them.)*

> *(As soon as our friends are out of sight,* **SIR GUY OF GISBOURNE** *enters. He is the Guy of Gisbourne we know from* The Adventures of Robin Hood, *a knight of the realm, a master swordsman, a sardonic wit, and the trickiest, sneakiest, most self-satisfied dandy who ever had a black heart and a pencil moustache. He wears a doublet and hose, and from his belt hangs a rapier that he sleeps with at night like a favorite pet. He has the plummy voice of a Shakespearean actor, and he rolls his r's better than Noël Coward. He is altogether reprehensible – yet wouldn't we all like to be him now and then.)*

> *(His sidekick is named* **MULCH,** *and he is a medieval peasant in training. He admires* **SIR GUY** *tremendously.)*

SIR GUY. *Mulch!*

MULCH. *(hurrying in)* Right here, Sir Guy. I'm back. I'm here. Hallo. Ha ha. It's me. *(sees the children in the audience)* Hello, nice to see you, thank you for coming. Are you comfy?

SIR GUY. Mulch! Stop talking to those sticky children and tell me what happened. Did you get it?

MULCH. *(who is not the fastest bloodhound in the pack)* "Get it"? Was I supposed to… "get" something, Sir Guy?

SIR GUY. The Naughty-and-Nice List? From the elves?

MULCH. Elves, sir?

SIR GUY. Happy little people with pointy ears. Not too bright.

> (**CALLIOPE** *jumps out from under the workbench with her fists clenched, but* **EMILY** *and* **AMOS** *restrain her.*)

MULCH. *(still groping)* "Not too bright…"

SIR GUY. The ones that we have locked in the Elfeterium. So you could threaten them and procure the Naughty-and-Nice List *do you remember now?!!*

MULCH. Oh right, right, right. Yes, yes, yes. Of course. Yes. No. I didn't get the list. I tried, but they wouldn't give it to me. And I asked them in the nicest way.

SIR GUY. You numbskull. You were supposed to threaten them. Now go back in there and paint them a picture of what will happen if they do not cooperate.

MULCH. I can't paint.

SIR GUY. A *mental* picture.

MULCH. Oh, I see. Oil or watercolor?

SIR GUY. Describe it to them and make them fear *for their very lives!*

MULCH. Oh. Right. Of course. That's it. And how do I do that again…?

SIR GUY. You tell them that if they do not hand over the Naughty-and-Nice List immediately, with dispatch, chop-chop, then tonight before bedtime, *their hot chocolate will be served cold! Haha!*

MULCH. Very sinister, sir. Anything else?

SIR GUY. They will go to bed at night wearing *scratchy pajamas!*

MULCH. Oh gasp. How could you.

SIR GUY. Made of *wool!*

MULCH. Excuse me, sir, but I believe that elves *like* wool at night, it keeps them warm.

SIR GUY. Don't bother me with details, I'm a big-idea man.

MULCH. Yes sir.

SIR GUY. They don't call me Guy of Gisbourne for nothing, you know. *(practicing with his sword)* Hya! Hya! Hya! Holy heavens I'm good with a sword. That comes from practice, Mulch. Always remember: Do what you love in life, then practice it until you're blue in the face. It builds character. Now what *I* love to do is splitting gizzards, and who could blame me?

MULCH. How do you mean, sir?

(Sad music plays, the melodramatic kind they used to play for silent films.)

SIR GUY. If you'll remember, Mulch, there was a time when I was Head Elf of this workshop.

MULCH. That's true, sir.

SIR GUY. I worked all day, every day, inventing toys, making toys, wrapping toys. Is it any wonder I got sick of toys?

MULCH. Well, sir –

SIR GUY. I made one little mistake and Santa demoted me to Apprentice. Apprentice, Mulch! He threw me like Lucifer from the sky to the earth, "O sing, O muse, Of man's First Disobedience and the Fruit / Of that Forbidden Tree!"

MULCH. Shakespeare?

SIR GUY. Milton.

MULCH. I didn't know his first name was Milton. And what was your mistake again?

SIR GUY. Oh it was nothing.

MULCH. Sir?

SIR GUY. Teeny, tiny …

MULCH. Which was?

SIR GUY. Oh, I stole Santa's sleigh and tried to sell it to Walmart. I thought I'd get a good price. But Santa caught me, he called me the Fallen Elf and demoted me and *now I want revenge!!*

MULCH. May I ask you a question, Sir Guy?

SIR GUY. Make it quick. Time's a-wasting.

MULCH. Why do you even want the Naughty-and-Nice List? What good will it do you?

SIR GUY. Ah, Mulch. You're such a mystery to me. Pretty face, but no brains. Now what is on the Naughty and Nice List, hm?

MULCH. Who's been naughty and who's been nice?

SIR GUY. And what else is on it?

MULCH. The children's Christmas lists?

SIR GUY. Exactly. And there are stores all over the world that would pay big money for that List! Ha! Mulch, you and I are going into business!

(sung to the tune of "Deck the Halls*")*

SIR GUY.
DECK THE HALLS WITH BOUGHS OF HOLLY,
FA LA LA LA LA, LA LA LA LAA!
SANTA CLAUS AIN'T FEELIN' JOLLY,
FA LA LA LA LA, LA LA LA LAA!

MULCH.
CHRISTMAS TIME WILL BE A PAIN, DEAR
FA LA LA, LA LA LA, LA, LA, LAA!
YOU WON'T SEE NO FLYIN' REINDEER
FA LA LA LA LA, LA LA LA LAA!

BOTH.
HOW WE LOVE TO COUNT OUR MONEY
FA LA LA LA LA, LA LA LA LAA!
CHRISTMAS ELVES AIN'T FEELIN' SUNNY
FA LA LA LA LA, LA LA LA LAA!

CHILDREN WEEPING, PARENTS PENSIVE,
FA LA LA, LA LA LA, LA, LA, LAA!
ALL THE TOYS WILL BE EXPENSIVE,
FA LA LA LA LA, LA LA LA LAA!

(dance)

MULCH.
ALL THE CHILDREN LOOK ASTOUNDED,
FA LA LA LA LA, LA LA LA LAA!

SIR GUY.
> RUDOLPH IS FOREVER GROUNDED,
> FA LA LA, LA LA LA, LA, LA, LAA!

BOTH.
> HOW YOU'LL MISS THOSE MOUNDS OF PRESENTS,
> FA LA LA LA LA, LA LA LA LAA!
> WE'LL BE KINGS AND YOU'LL BE PEASANTS,
> FA LA LA LA LA,
> LA LA,
> LA,
> LAAAAAAAAAAAA!

> *(Big ending in harmony.* **SIR GUY** *and* **MULCH** *run off together. The three friends emerge from behind the doll house.)*

CALLIOPE. Oh my gosh! How did this happen?!

EMILY. Do you know him?

CALLIOPE. Of course I know him. He was one of us, an elf. But he was always ambitious. He thought *he* should be running the place, not Santa. But now we've got to act fast. Amos, you go find Santa and tell him what's happened. He'll be in his rooms getting dressed for the Ride.

AMOS. Yes *sir!*

> *(***AMOS*** *runs off.)*

CALLIOPE. Emily, you and I have to go see the elves.

EMILY. But how can we? He said they're locked in the Elfeterium.

CALLIOPE. We'll infiltrate. There are air ducts at both ends of the room. You'll take one, I'll take the other. I think we're small enough to squeeze through. Come on!

> *(They start to run out, but* **CALLIOPE** *stops.)*

Wait! Elf cheer!

EMILY. Elf cheer?

CALLIOPE. We may be small
> And smelly, too,

But elves
Themselves
Are strong and true!

EMILY. We may be small
And smelly, too,
But elves
Themselves
Are strong and true!

CALLIOPE. *(to the kids in the audience)* Kids! Quick! We need your help! This side!

(She leads one side of the audience.)

We may be small
And smelly, too,
But elves
Themselves
Are strong and true!

EMILY. Now this side!
We may be small
And smelly, too,
But elves
Themselves
Are strong and true!

BOTH. *All together now!*
We may be small
And smelly, too,
But elves
Themselves
Are strong and true!

EMILY. Let's go!

(They run off. Beat. Then **AMOS OF KANSAS,** *the twin brother of our* **AMOS,** *enters carrying a suitcase. For clarity's sake, for the rest of the play, we'll call them "Amos of Kansas" and "Amos". Despite what* **AMOS** *said about being handsomer than* **AMOS OF KANSAS,** *they are in fact identical. [Note: they're played by the same actor.]*

We can tell them apart by their clothes, their accents and their attitudes: **AMOS OF KANSAS** *wears a bow-tie and a straw hat; he has a strong Midwestern twang in his speech; and he's very relaxed and philosophical about life.)*

(When **AMOS OF KANSAS** *walks into the room, he puts down his suitcase, looks around and scratches his head.)*

AMOS OF KANSAS. Gal dang it. If this ain't crazy, then I'm the back end of a donkey pullin' a bale o' hay. My brother Amos invited me to his place for the holidays, but when I got there all the way from Kansas he'd flown the coop. Then I found this here letter from a gal named Emily, and she says

(He pulls out a letter and starts to read it.)

"Ylreir – Belcnuraed …"

(He realizes that the letter is upside down and turns it around and starts again.)

"Dear Uncle Brierly,"

which is odd right there because I ain't her uncle and I ain't named Brierly.

"Dear Uncle Brierly. Do not worry about me. I have gone to the North Pole with Amos to save Christmas. Emily."

So my twin brother Amos is up here on some hair-brained scheme, which means he's in trouble, and I'm here to get him out of it. I'm what you might call my brother's keeper. Ya see, the Good Book asks "Am I my brother's keeper?" to which the answer is yes, you should be. We all gotta look out for each other in this world 'cause everybody needs a helpin' hand now and then. As the poet said, "No mouse is an island."

(At which point, **EMILY** *runs on carrying a snow globe, talking a mile a minute. She thinks he's* **AMOS.***)*

EMILY. Oh, Amos! Amos, thank goodness I found you, I got the Naughty-and-Nice List from the elves, you see they had it like Calliope said they would and they *trusted* me because they said I had a kind and beautiful face and now I love every single one of them but then that awful man Sir Guy of Gisbourne saw me escaping and now he's after me and I have to hide the List!

SIR GUY. *(off) Young lady, get back here!*

EMILY. Quick, here, you take the List, it's hidden at the bottom of this snow globe and you'll have to guard it with your life while I distract them, so quick, go hide someplace and whatever you do, don't let Guy of Gisbourne have it 'cause that would be the end of Christmas for every child in the entire world and it would be *us* that would be responsible and then I'd never sleep again for a single night in my entire life!!

(**AMOS OF KANSAS** *just looks at the audience.*)

EMILY. Wait! Maybe you're right. I *can* run faster than you, so I'll keep the List for now and you distract them. As soon as they're gone, I'll be back. Okay? Good. And let me say you're being very brave and I'm immensely proud of you.

(*She kisses him on the cheek and runs off.*)

AMOS OF KANSAS. I gotta say, these people up north are mighty friendly.

(*At which moment,* **SIR GUY** *runs in.*)

SIR GUY. Where did she go, I was on her trail and now she's… (*He sees* **AMOS OF KANSAS**.) Who are you? Are you an elf?

AMOS OF KANSAS. Nope.

SIR GUY. Are you a reindeer?

AMOS OF KANSAS. Nope.

SIR GUY. What are you then?

AMOS OF KANSAS. Mouse.

SIR GUY. A mouse?

AMOS OF KANSAS. Yup.

SIR GUY. Well, Mousey, who was that girl who ran through this room just now? Do you know her?

AMOS OF KANSAS. Nope.

SIR GUY. You've never seen her before?

AMOS OF KANSAS. Nope.

SIR GUY. Oh, please. You mean she didn't give you a list to hold which you are now hiding somewhere about your little mousey person?

AMOS OF KANSAS. ...Nope.

SIR GUY. Well I think you're *fibbing!* I think you're trying to protect her *and* the Naughty-and-Nice List, which I believe I see bulging out of your front pocket at this very moment *(He sees the letter, not the list, but thinks it's the list.)* and so I'm afraid I have to insist that you *hand it over to me this instant!!*

(**AMOS OF KANSAS** *calmly takes the pair of gloves that are hanging over* **SIR GUY**'s *belt and slaps* **SIR GUY** *across the face with them – then hands them back to* **SIR GUY**.)

AMOS OF KANSAS. *(calmly)* Never call a Midwesterner a fibber.

(**SIR GUY** *is so apoplectic he's almost speechless.*)

SIR GUY. *Do you see this sword?! She's called Old Betsy and when I return you will dance to her tune until Rudolph the Reindeer starts having grandchildren!!*

(**SIR GUY** *stomps off – and the moment he's gone,* **EMILY** *runs back on.*)

EMILY. Is he gone? Good job. Now here's the List and you know what to do with it. Go hide while I find Santa and Calliope and tell them the List is safe and it's okay to get ready for the Ride, how does that sound?

AMOS OF KANSAS. ...Purty good.

EMILY. You're amazing.

(*She kisses him on the cheek.*)

MULCH. *(off) Sir, I see the mouse and the girl and I'm closing in!*
EMILY. *Quick! Go!*

> (**AMOS OF KANSAS** *and* **EMILY** *run off in opposite directions, left and right, and the instant they're gone,* **SANTA CLAUS** *comes in straight down center.)*

> (*Yes. Santa. He looks exactly as we dream about him, with a red suit, a big belly and a white beard; and yet he's not a stereotype. He's interesting and he has a temper.*)

SANTA CLAUS. What the blazes is going on around here?! I can't find the elves, my bag isn't packed, there's a lunatic with a sword running around my workshop and in less than fifteen minutes I begin my rounds! *Rudolph! Blitzen!*

> (**EMILY** *runs in almost knocking* **SANTA CLAUS** *over.)*

Ah!

EMILY. Oh, sir, I'm very sorry I…

> (*She looks up and sees that it's* **SANTA CLAUS** *and her mouth drops open.)*

Santa Claus! It's you! Is it really you?!

SANTA CLAUS. It was last time I checked.

> (**SANTA CLAUS** *sits down, and instinctively* **EMILY** *sits on his knee as she talks to him.)*

EMILY. Oh my gosh would I love to stay and talk and have some hot chocolate together with the little marshmallows on top, but I have a job to do. I have to save Christmas.

SANTA CLAUS. *Save Christmas?!*

> (*At which point* **CALLIOPE** *runs in.)*

CALLIOPE. Santa! There you are!

> (*She sits on* **SANTA CLAUS'S** *other knee.* **SANTA CLAUS** *has that effect on people. And elves. To* **EMILY***:)*

Did you get the List?!

EMILY. I did, but I gave it to Amos to hide because they're after me!

CALLIOPE. Okay, I'll find Amos, get the List from him, give it to Santa and we're off on the Ride. Santa, stay here for your own safety.

(**CALLIOPE** *runs off.*)

SANTA CLAUS. My own safety?! Who's running this show? Calliope, get back here!

(**SANTA CLAUS** *marches off after* **CALLIOPE**, *leaving* **EMILY** *alone on stage — at which point* **AMOS** *enters, looking for* **SANTA CLAUS**.)

AMOS. Santa...? San-ta...?

EMILY. Amos! What are you doing here? I told you to hide!

AMOS. You did? I thought you told me to find Santa.

EMILY. That was before I found the Naughty-and-Nice List.

AMOS. You found the List?!

EMILY. Of course I found it! Don't be silly! But I think *I* should keep it now because Santa's almost ready to go on his rounds and I think I can slip it to him better than you can as long as you distract Sir Guy and Mulch, so hand it over.

AMOS. ...Hand what over?

EMILY. The Naughty-and-Nice List! You didn't lose it, did you? *(shaking him)* Amos, tell me you didn't lose the Naughty-and-Nice List!

MULCH. *(off) There she is, Sir Guy! I see her!*

SIR GUY. *(off) I see her, too! You go in from the South, I'll come from the North and we'll get her in a pincer movement!*

EMILY. Oh, no, he's back! All right, you keep the List but don't let him have it no matter what, you *promised!*

(*She runs off.* **AMOS** *is speechless. Then* **SIR GUY** *enters.*)

SIR GUY. Well, well, well. I've been looking for you.

AMOS. You have?

SIR GUY. And I've brought Old Betsy with me.

AMOS. You mean your wife?

SIR GUY. Don't be funny!

AMOS. Your cow?

SIR GUY. You think you're brave, don't you? Do you prefer pistols or swords?

AMOS. Pistols?

SIR GUY. No. Swords. I'm better with swords. And I've brought you one, too. There. Now defend yourself!

(He tosses **AMOS** *a sword and starts dueling with him.* **AMOS** *is terrified and holds the sword with both hands, slashing with his eyes closed, crying out with each slash. The swords clang furiously.)*

Hya! Hya! Hya!

AMOS. *Ah! Ah! Ah!*

Ayeeee!

*(***AMOS*** runs off with* **SIR GUY** *in hot pursuit. A chase sequence ensues. Keystone Cops-type music plays and all our friends run in and out as parts of the various chases.)*

(Note: Every time **MULCH** *appears, he has a big frying pan with him and waves it and cries "Stand and deliver!" to whomever he's chasing.)*

(First, **AMOS** *runs through being chased by* **SIR GUY**. *"Help, help, help, help, help, help!" "Stand still, you coward!")*

(Second, **CALLIOPE** *runs through being chased by* **MULCH**. *"Stand and deliver!")*

(Third, **SIR GUY** *runs through being chased by* **AMOS OF KANSAS**. *"Get back here, you varmint!")*

(Fourth, **EMILY** *runs through being chased by* **MULCH**. *"Stand and deliver!" "Ahhhhhhhh!")*

(Fifth, **AMOS** *runs in, still being chased by* **SIR GUY**. *"Old Betsy is getting impatient!" "You should try milking*

her!" **AMOS** *drops his sword and runs off, leaving* **SIR GUY** *alone on stage.)*

(Then **MULCH** *runs on and sees* **SIR GUY**, *but only from the back.)*

MULCH. *(poking* **SIR GUY** *in the back with his frying pan)* Stand and deliver! Put your hands up! And don't turn around!

SIR GUY. *(His hands up, not turning around.)* It's me, you half-wit. Sir Guy.

MULCH. Oh really? Or are you an elf dressed up as Sir Guy to try and fool me in front of the entire population of the North Pole, eh? Ha? Hanh?!

*(*SIR GUY *turns around just as* MULCH *tries to bean him with the frying pan. They both get hit on the nose with it and both cry out in pain.)*

SIR GUY. *Ow! You nincompoop!*

MULCH. Ah! Sorry, sorry, sorry, sorry, sorry, sorry…

SIR GUY. *You could have knocked my head off!*

MULCH. Sorry, sorry, sorry. But did you get the Naughty-and-Nice List?

SIR GUY. *No!* I'll have it any second if that ridiculous mouse will stand still!

MULCH. I'll get him for you!

*(*MULCH *runs off. At which point* AMOS OF KANSAS *enters but* SIR GUY *doesn't see him.)*

SIR GUY. He's a coward! And a weakling! I'll split him from the knobs to the chops! The narrows to the bottom! From stem to sternum! Ha!

(He sees **AMOS OF KANSAS**.*)*

Well, well, well, look who's here: The Last of the Mouse-hicans. Have you come to surrender, is that it? Hya, hya, hya! "Who are these mice who are so fond of death?"

*(*AMOS OF KANSAS *picks up the sword that* AMOS *dropped.)*

AMOS OF KANSAS. Ah hate to do this to ya, but sword fightin' is a sort o' specialty o' mine.

SIR GUY. Oh, pul-ease. Spare me the bravado. Your only specialty appears to be "Running from Danger." Ha! *En garde!*

AMOS OF KANSAS. Some people just don't listen.

(Sword fight. The music is from Korngold's score to the 1939 movie Robin Hood. During the fight, MULCH runs off.)

(It's a wonderful fight and we soon see that AMOS OF KANSAS wasn't boasting: He's a masterful swordsman. By the end, SIR GUY is fighting for his life.)

SIR GUY. Please! Stop! I beg you!

(At which point EMILY and CALLIOPE rush on.)

EMILY. Oh my gosh!

CALLIOPE. What happened?!

EMILY. What's going on?!

AMOS OF KANSAS. This here villain just won't take no for an answer. Now are ya sorry?

SIR GUY. Yes! Yes! I'm terribly sorry! I cower, I grovel, I beg your forgiveness.

AMOS OF KANSAS. Well ya can't say fairer than that. I spare ya.

(He puts up his sword.)

EMILY. Amos, what happened? You don't even sound like yourself.

CALLIOPE. *(to EMILY)* He looks a little different too. He's not as handsome.

EMILY. *(to CALLIOPE, in love)* I think he's very handsome.

AMOS OF KANSAS. This place is the gal durndest, craziest, wildest nuthouse I ever seen, and I'm goin' home.

EMILY. Amos, you can't go! Wait! You have the Naughty-and-Nice List, and we need it if we're going to save Christmas!

AMOS OF KANSAS. You mean this? Here. It's all yours. *(He *tosses it to them.)* Seems like a lot o' trouble to me.

CALLIOPE & EMILY. Yay!

SIR GUY. Ah!

AMOS OF KANSAS. See ya round. If ya ever get to Kansas, stop by and say hello.

(He exits.)

EMILY & CALLIOPE. …Kansas?

EMILY. Why would he say K – …

(**EMILY** *and* **CALLIOPE** *look at each other. They get it.)*

Oh my gosh! Is that Amos's *brother* – ?

CALLIOPE. It must be.

EMILY. *Amos, wait! We want to talk to you!*

CALLIOPE. *There's been a mistake! Come back!*

AMOS OF KANSAS. *(off – the speech is long to let the actor playing Amos/Amos change and move to his next entrance so that it feels like there really are two different mice)* I ain't comin' back fer nobody! This here place is crazy! I said to my mama, "They can't all be crazy back East, they gotta have a few normal people," but she says, "No they ain't normal, they are nuttier than fruitcakes." [And she was right. And it seems to me that the North Pole just makes you nuttier'n ever. So I'm headin' back to the place I know best and I wish you well, so good-bye.]*

(At which moment, **AMOS** *runs in from the other side of the stage. He's panting hard.)*

AMOS. Okay, I think I lost him, but I'm just too tired to run any *Ah!*

---

*The bracketed dialogue is there in case the actor playing **AMOS/ AMOS OF KANSAS** needs the extra time to get around behind the set to his entrance. The offstage dialogue should be recorded and played from one side of the stage (where **AMOS OF KANSAS** exited) with the other **AMOS** entering from the opposite side. Use as much or little of this speech as necessary to do the stage trick. The less the better. It would be ideal if the line can end with "fruitcakes" and then have a full-fledged **AMOS** run into the room from the other side of the stage.

(He has seen **SIR GUY** *and is frightened. But* **SIR GUY** *thinks there's only one* **AMOS** *and he does a double-take – and then he starts groveling.)*

SIR GUY. *Ah! Please, please spare me! Whatever game you're playing, I admit defeat! You're a miraculous mouse! A marvelous wee beastie and my hat is off to you!*

*(***AMOS*** stares at him in disbelief…when* **SANTA CLAUS** *enters.)*

SANTA CLAUS. What the devil is going on around here?

AMOS. *(mouth agape)* …*Santa Claus!*

CALLIOPE. Hi, Santa.

EMILY. Hello, Santa.

SANTA CLAUS. Where is everybody? Where are my elves? What's going on?

EMILY. Well, Santa, these two men here locked up all the elves and actually threatened them if they wouldn't give up the –

AMOS. I was sitting at home making cookies hoping that you'd come this year and then this elf arrived and took me to the –

CALLIOPE. They wanted the Naughty and Nice List and locked the elves in the Elfiterium!, so Emily and I had to sneak in there and –

SANTA CLAUS. *STOP!* I can't understand a word you're saying and I – … *(He sees* **SIR GUY.***)* Ralphie! What are you doing here?

RALPHIE, FORMERLY KNOWN AS SIR GUY. Well, sir, I think I made a teensy-tiny little mistake…

SANTA CLAUS. Walmart again?

RALPHIE. No, sir. Bloomingdale's. I'm moving up in the world. You see, I thought you might want to share the Naughty and Nice List with some friendly retailers, only in the spirit of Christmas, of course –

SANTA CLAUS. Ralph-ie…

RALPHIE. Oh all right, I was going to sell it. But now I see the error of my ways and I would like to come back to the Workshop again, if you can forgive me? Can you? Please?

SANTA CLAUS. *(beat; then with a sign of good fellowship)* ...Yes, of course I can. Forgiveness is what this season is all about. The important thing is to try harder next time.

RALPHIE. Oh I will, I promise!

SANTA CLAUS. Good. You can go now.

(RALPHIE exits.)

Now *I'd* better go. The Ride starts soon.

CALLIOPE. "Soon"?! Santa, it starts in two minutes!

SANTA CLAUS. Two minutes?! Why didn't you say so?! *(patting his suit)* Now let's see, I seem to have misplaced the Naughty-and-Nice List... *(He sees it in EMILY's hand and takes it from her.)* Oh there it is. You know young lady you shouldn't just pick things up whenever you please. This is very valuable.

(AMOS, EMILY and CALLIOPE are about to react, but SANTA CLAUS cuts them off:)

Now you two need to be in your beds so I can leave you your presents.

AMOS. Presents?! Yippee! We're gettin' presents! I want a squirt gun and a cowboy hat and a scooter and a –

SANTA CLAUS. Now, now, let's not overdo it. When you think about it, you've already received a present this year.

AMOS. I have?

SANTA CLAUS. Of course you have.

(Christmas music starts to play, something warm and inspiring.)

The best Christmas presents don't come in packages, Amos. They involve the heart. They are things like courage and kindness, honesty and love. You, my friend, have had an adventure. And if you don't make life an adventure, what's the use? You never change, you never grow. Now we have some presentations to make. Calliope.

CALLIOPE. I'm on it.

*(The music changes. **CALLIOPE** steps forward with two ribbon necklaces with a medal hanging from each one.)*

SANTA CLAUS. This for Emily. The North Pole Medal for Wit and Bravery Beyond the Call of Duty. You helped save Christmas and we are all grateful.

EMILY. Thank you, sir.

SANTA CLAUS. And this for Amos. The North Pole Medal for Adventurer First Class. Congratulations.

AMOS. Thank you, sir.

*(**CALLIOPE** coughs)*

CALLIOPE. Santa, it's midnight.

SANTA CLAUS. Midnight?! Then it's time for the Ride! Now where's my sack?! Where's my hat?! *And where are my reindeer?!!*

(The music becomes triumphant and exciting – and turns into a rap song:)

SANTA CLAUS.

NOW DASHER, NOW DANCER,
NOW PRANCER IS FIXIN'
TO JUMP INTO THE SKY
WITH A DEER NAMED VIXEN.
ON COMET! ON CUPID!
NOW IT'S TIME TO MOVE ALONG
WITH MISTER DONNER, MISTER BLITZEN
WHILE I'M SINGIN' THIS SONG.

*(**SANTA CLAUS** goes while the others continue. As they sing, the stage is transformed back into Amos and Emily's house.)*

EMILY, AMOS & CALLIOPE.

TO THE TOP OF THE PORCH!
AND TO THE TOP OF THE WALL!
NOW JUMP WITH A BUMP

WHILE YOU DASH AWAY ALL!
DASH
DASH
DASH
DASH
DASH AWAY ALL!

EMILY.

HE WAS DRESSED ALL IN FUR,
WITH A PACK FULL OF LOOT,
AND IT HAD TO BE HOT
INSIDE THAT CHRISTMAS SUIT.
WITH THE FUR AND THE HAT
AND THE GLOVES AND THE BOOT
AND HIS CLOTHES WERE ALL TARNISHED
WITH ASHES AND SOOOT.

ALL.

"SOOOT"?

EMILY.

"SOOOT"!

CALLIOPE.

A BUNDLE OF TOYS
HE HAD FLUNG ON HIS BACK
AND HE LOOKED
LIKE A BOOK
AND A PEDDLAR
NOT A MEDDLER
WITH A PACK
GETTIN' FLAK
BACKPACK
BACK PACK,
BACK PACK
WITH HIS TOYS
MAKIN' NOISE
WHEN HE OPENED UP HIS SACK!

AMOS.

HIS EYES HOW THEY TWINKLED!
HIS DIMPLES HOW MERRY!
LIKE A VERY MERRY CHERRY

AND HIS EYES LIKE A BERRY
AND HIS BEARD IS KINDA HAIRY
BUT HE NEVER LOOKS SCARY
BUT HE COULD
IN THE WOOD
IF HE MET A POLAR BEARY.

ALL.
HE WAS CHUBBY AND PLUMP,
SITS DOWN WITH A BUMP,
WITH A NOD AND A WINK,
IT KINDA MAKES YOU WANNA THINK:
WHO IS
THIS MAN?
A RIGHT
JOLLY OLD ELF
HIMSELF
THAT'S THE MAN
WITH THE TAN
AND THE LOOT
WITH THE BOOT
DOESN'T EAT ENOUGH FRUIT,
BUT HE'S JOLLY
WITH THE HOLLY,
MAKES US HAPPY
LIKE OUR PAPPY
AND OUR MOM
AND OUR GRAN
AND THE REST OF THE CLAN.
THERE'S THE SANDMAN,
TOOTH FAIRY,
NEVER SCARY,
EASTER BUNNY,
HE'S A HONEY,
BUT THERE'S NOTHIN' CLOSE
NOTHIN' LIKE
WON'T YOU DRIVE OUR SLEIGH TONIGHT
NOTHIN' LIKE HIM BECAUSE
HE'S SANTA CLAUS!

(End of song. **AMOS** *and* **EMILY** *exit, stretching and rubbing their eyes.* **CALLIOPE** *looks out at the audience and winks – and throws a handful of sparkly fairy dust into the air, then exits with a wonderful smile as it shimmers to the ground.* **UNCLE BRIERLY** *enters with an armful of presents.)*

UNCLE BRIERLY. *(on a recording, as the man himself puts presents under the tree)* He spoke not a word, but went straight to his work,
And filled all the stockings, then turned with a jerk.
And laying his finger aside of his nose,
And giving a nod, up the chimney he rose!

(Bells of all kinds. And sunlight. It's morning!)

UNCLE BRIERLY. *(speaking now)* Emily! Amos! It's Christmas morning!

*(***EMILY*** hurries in, rubbing her eyes – and sees the tree and the presents and starts calling with excitement:)*

EMILY. Amos! Amos, wake up! It's Christmas!

AMOS. *(still sleepy)* Huh…what…Christmas morning? Yippee! Oh, thank you Santa Claus!

*(As **AMOS** continues his excitement about Christmas, **EMILY** goes into a reverie. She's starting to remember what happened last night.)*

EMILY. Santa Claus…?

AMOS. I want my stocking! Where's my stocking?! Oh I hope I got some presents this year. I've tried to be a good mouse, I really have. I've cleaned my room, I've cleaned my plate, I've cleaned my ears – they had a lot of wax in 'em –

EMILY. Oh, Amos, I had the most beautiful dream last night. I dreamt that I was in Santa's Workshop and that you and I somehow…saved Christmas…

AMOS. Saved Christmas? That's ridiculous. How could you and I… Wait a second. I think I just had the same dream. There were gumdrops and lollipops and I met an elf… *(he sighs)* Too bad it never happened.

EMILY. Yeah, too bad…

> (*Then* **EMILY** *looks down and notices the medal hanging around her neck.*)

EMILY. …Amos.

AMOS. Yeah?

EMILY. I want you to look down very slowly.

> (**AMOS** *looks down slowly…and he gets it. They look at each other with their mouths open.*)

UNCLE BRIERLY. Have you two looked in your stockings yet?

EMILY & AMOS. Not yet! / Let's see! / Oh look! / Look at this! / Here it is! / Oh boy, oh boy, oh boy, oh boy!

UNCLE BRIERLY. And I found this odd-looking contraption under the tree. I wonder who this is for?

AMOS. My squirt gun! Oh my gosh. And it even has water in it!

> (*And he turns to the audience and shoots water in a semi-circle right onto the kids.*)

> YIPPEE!

UNCLE BRIERLY. He sprang to his sleigh, to his team gave a whistle,

And away they all flew like the down on a thistle.

But I heard him exclaim, 'ere he drove out of sight:

SANTA CLAUS. (*off*) "MERRY CHRISTMAS TO ALL,

ALL. AND TO ALL A GOOD NIGHT!"

> (**SANTA CLAUS** *and* **CALLIOPE** *reenter and everyone sings Deck the Halls – the right way!*)

> (*curtain*)

ABOUT THE AUTHOR

KEN LUDWIG is an internationally acclaimed playwright who has had six shows on Broadway and six in the West End. He has received two Laurence Olivier Awards (England's highest theatre honor), three Tony Award nominations, two Helen Hayes Awards, and his work has been commissioned by The Royal Shakespeare Company. *The Game's Afoot; or Holmes for the Holidays* won the Edgar Alan Poe Award for Best Mystery of 2012. *Crazy For You* won the Olivier and Tony Awards as Best Musical. *Lend Me A Tenor*, which won two Tony Awards and the Olivier nomination for Comedy of the Year, was called "one of the two great farces by a living writer" by *The New York Times*. Other Broadway and West End shows include *Twentieth Century* starring Alec Baldwin and Anne Heche, *Moon Over Buffalo* starring Carol Burnett, Lynn Redgrave, Joan Collins and Frank Langella, *The Adventures of Tom Sawyer*, and *Treasure Island* (Theatre Royal, Haymarket; AATE Distinguished Play Award). *Shakespeare in Hollywood* was commissioned by The Royal Shakespeare Company and won the Helen Hayes Award as Best Play. Other plays and musicals include *Leading Ladies, Be My Baby, The Beaux' Stratagem* (adaptation with Thornton Wilder at the request of the Wilder Estate), *The Three Musketeers* (Bristol Old Vic), *An American in Paris, The Fox on the Fairway, Midsummer/Jersey*, and *Baskerville*. His work has appeared in *The Yale Review* and he has written a book for Random House entitled *How To Teach Your Children Shakespeare*. He studied music at Harvard with Leonard Bernstein and theatre history at Cambridge University, and he is on the Board of Governors of the Folger Shakespeare Library in Washington, D.C. For more information please visit www.kenludwig.com.

Also by
Ken Ludwig…

Be My Baby

The Beaux Stratagem

The Fox on the Fairway

The Game's Afoot

Leading Ladies

Lend Me A Tenor

Midsummer/Jersey

Moon Over Buffalo

Postmortem

Shakespeare in Hollywood

Sullivan & Gilbert

The Three Musketeers

Treasure Island

Twentieth Century

Please visit our website **samuelfrench.com** for complete descriptions and licensing information.